STAR WARS®

REVENGE OF THE SITH™
THE MOVIE STORYBOOK

A STORYBOOK ADAPTED BY
ALICE ALFONSI

BASED ON THE STORY AND SCREENPLAY BY
GEORGE LUCAS

LUCAS
BOOKS

■SCHOLASTIC

Special thanks to the following people
for their work on this book.

At Lucasfilm Ltd.:
Amy Gary, Director of Publishing
Linda Kelly, Editor
Sue Rostoni, Managing Editor
Iain Morris, Art Editor
Leland Chee, Keeper of the Holocron

At Random House Children's Books:
Lisa Findlay, Associate Editor
Thomas Velázquez, Designer
Godwin Chu, Copy Editor
Alison Gervais, Production Manager

Scholastic Children's Books, Commonwealth House, 1-19 New Oxford Street, London WC1A 1NU. A division of Scholastic Ltd.

First published in the USA by Random House Children's Books, a division of Random House, Inc., New York, 2005

This edition first published in the UK by Scholastic Ltd, 2005

1 2 3 4 5 6 7 8 9 10. Printed by Proost, Belgium

www.starwars.com

A long time ago in a galaxy far, far away. . . .

War! The Republic is crumbling
under attacks by the ruthless
Sith Lord Count Dooku.
There are heroes on both sides.
Evil is everywhere.

In a stunning move, the fiendish
droid leader, General Grievous,
has swept into the Republic
capital and kidnapped
Chancellor Palpatine, leader of
the Galactic Senate.

As the Separatist droid army
attempts to flee the besieged
capital with their valuable
hostage, two Jedi Knights lead a
desperate mission to rescue the
captive Chancellor. . . .

"**F**lying is for droids!" cried Jedi Master Obi-Wan Kenobi. He and the young Jedi Knight Anakin Skywalker maneuvered their starfighters through a barrage of laser fire.

Circling like bats, enemy fighters protected a mammoth battle cruiser dead ahead. The Jedi were determined to board that ship and arrest General Grievous before he could flee with his prisoner.

Rocketing through space, the Jedi dodged battleship laser bolts and vulture droids. Droid tri-fighters swarmed the Jedi's starfighters, and spider-like buzz droids landed on their hulls.

"First Jedi rule," Obi-Wan told Anakin. "Survive!"

Obi-Wan barely made it through the onslaught. But his friend and former apprentice was one of the most powerful and gifted young Jedi ever to be trained. Anakin easily evaded the danger and came to his Master's aid.

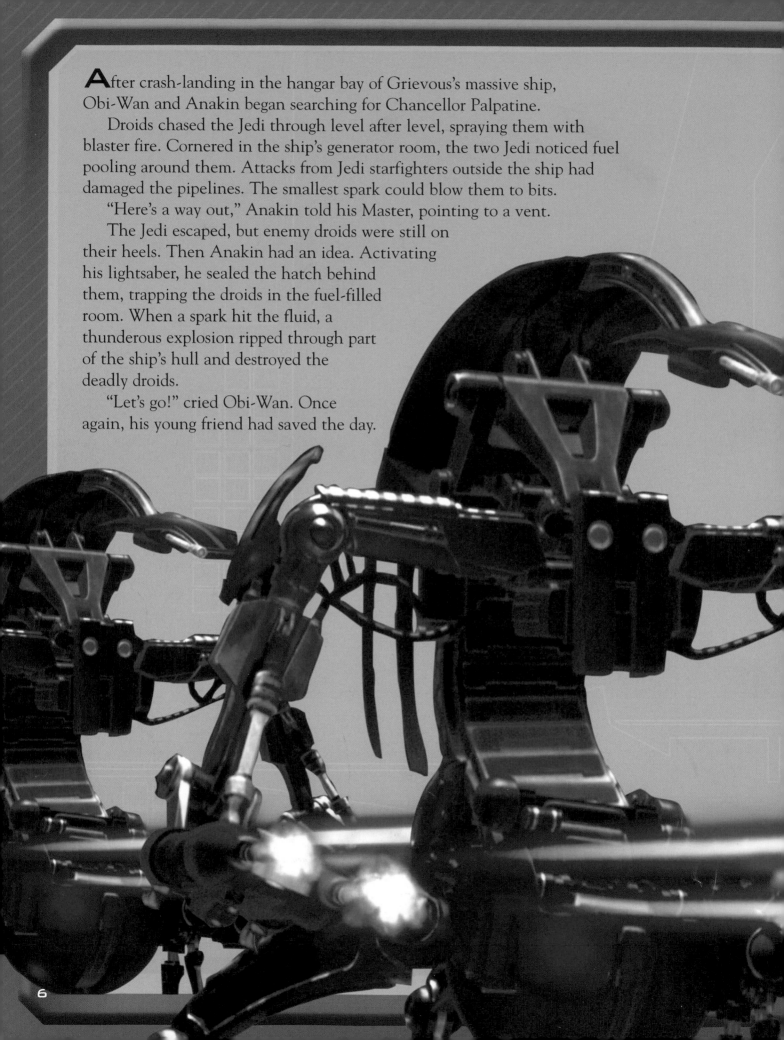

After crash-landing in the hangar bay of Grievous's massive ship, Obi-Wan and Anakin began searching for Chancellor Palpatine.

Droids chased the Jedi through level after level, spraying them with blaster fire. Cornered in the ship's generator room, the two Jedi noticed fuel pooling around them. Attacks from Jedi starfighters outside the ship had damaged the pipelines. The smallest spark could blow them to bits.

"Here's a way out," Anakin told his Master, pointing to a vent.

The Jedi escaped, but enemy droids were still on their heels. Then Anakin had an idea. Activating his lightsaber, he sealed the hatch behind them, trapping the droids in the fuel-filled room. When a spark hit the fluid, a thunderous explosion ripped through part of the ship's hull and destroyed the deadly droids.

"Let's go!" cried Obi-Wan. Once again, his young friend had saved the day.

With the help of Anakin's astromech droid, R2-D2, the Jedi finally located Chancellor Palpatine in General Grievous's quarters. Guarding him was a familiar enemy—the dangerous Sith Lord Darth Tyranus, known throughout the galaxy as Count Dooku.

Once a Jedi Master, Dooku had left the Jedi Order to serve the dark side and lead the Separatists' war against the Republic. The last time he'd fought Obi-Wan and Anakin, he'd wounded them both. He would have killed them, too, if Jedi Master Yoda hadn't come to the rescue.

Seeing their old opponent, Obi-Wan and Anakin threw off their cloaks and ignited their lightsabers. "You will not escape us this time, Dooku," Obi-Wan said.

The Sith Lord sneered. "Just because there are two of you, do not assume you have the advantage."

Together, Obi-Wan and Anakin charged. Lightsaber blades humming, the two Jedi slashed and lunged, struggling against the Sith Lord's masterful swordplay.

"Your moves are clumsy, Kenobi . . . too predictable," Dooku taunted as he parried blow after blow with his curved-handled lightsaber.

All three combatants spun, kicked, and struck with electric speed. Using the Force, Dooku threw Obi-Wan against a wall, knocking him unconscious.

Anakin continued the fight alone, desperate to find an advantage. From across the room, Chancellor Palpatine advised, "Use your aggressive feelings, Anakin. Call on your rage. Focus it, or you don't stand a chance against him."

Anakin's Jedi mentors had taught him to always reject the emotions of anger, fear, and hate. A true Jedi shunned these things. But Anakin was listening to Palpatine's urging, and he attacked Dooku with savage fury.

Anakin gained the advantage through his mad, relentless assault. He cut off Count Dooku's right hand, seized the Dark Lord's crimson weapon, and held two laser blades at Dooku's throat.

In a plea for mercy, the Sith Lord looked to the Chancellor with desperate eyes. But Palpatine ignored the plea and commanded Anakin to destroy Dooku. Giving in to his rage and hate, Anakin killed the Sith Lord. Only afterward did the young Jedi regret his decision.

"He was an unarmed prisoner," Anakin murmured with shame. "I shouldn't have done that. It's not the Jedi way."

The Chancellor brushed off Anakin's words. "You did well," he said.

Suddenly a blast rocked Grievous's command ship. The earlier fuel explosion in the generator room had made the battle cruiser unstable. Now the hull was breaking apart!

Anakin rushed to Obi-Wan's side.

"Leave him," urged Palpatine, "or we'll never make it."

This time, Anakin did not obey the Chancellor. "His fate will be the same as ours," Anakin declared as he lifted Obi-Wan.

Anakin led the Chancellor to the hangar bay, but every one of the fighters was too damaged to fly.

By now, Obi-Wan had regained consciousness. "We'll head toward the bridge and see if we can find an escape pod," he said.

As they raced down the hall, a deadly ray shield dropped in front of them. More shields dropped until they were trapped in a laser cage!

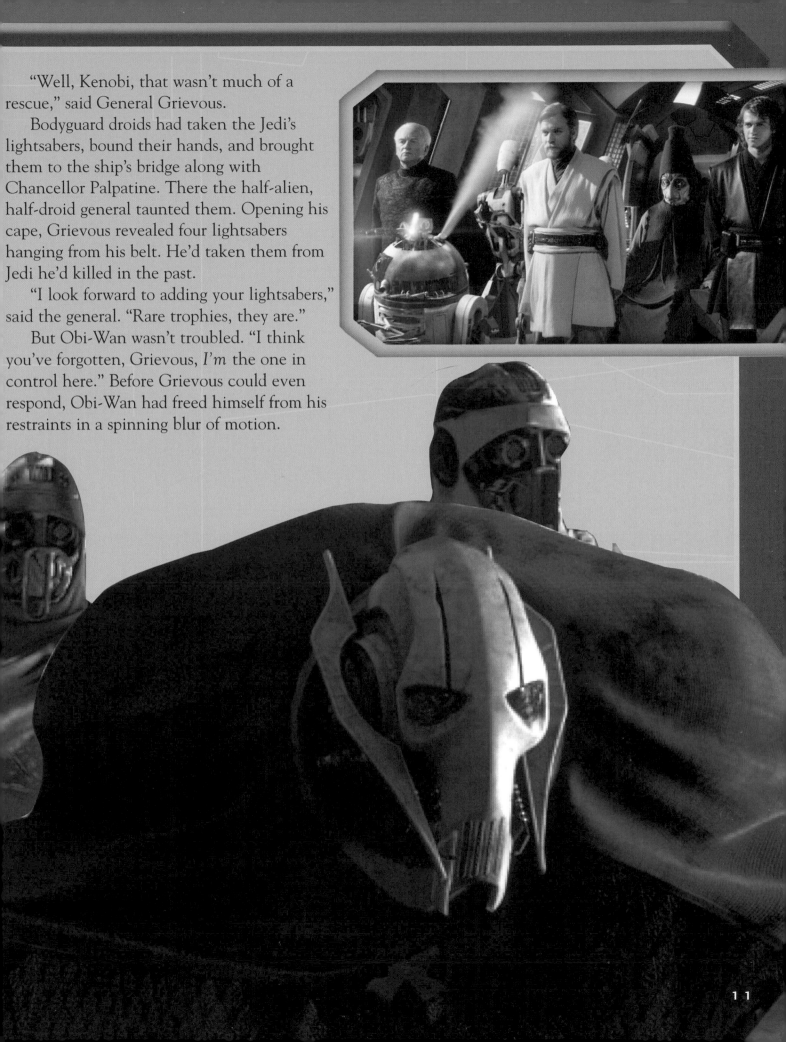

"Well, Kenobi, that wasn't much of a rescue," said General Grievous.

Bodyguard droids had taken the Jedi's lightsabers, bound their hands, and brought them to the ship's bridge along with Chancellor Palpatine. There the half-alien, half-droid general taunted them. Opening his cape, Grievous revealed four lightsabers hanging from his belt. He'd taken them from Jedi he'd killed in the past.

"I look forward to adding your lightsabers," said the general. "Rare trophies, they are."

But Obi-Wan wasn't troubled. "I think you've forgotten, Grievous, *I'm* the one in control here." Before Grievous could even respond, Obi-Wan had freed himself from his restraints in a spinning blur of motion.

Using the Force, Obi-Wan pulled his own lightsaber from the general's grip and began striking down Grievous's bodyguard droids. Anakin joined his Master in the fight, and the two Jedi soon had the advantage.

Just then, alarms sounded and the huge ship violently shifted. The cruiser was falling out of orbit!

General Grievous wasted no time saving himself. He rushed to the escape pod bay. He jettisoned every last pod before launching himself into space. Now the Jedi and the Chancellor were trapped on a crashing ship!

Obi-Wan could see only one way out of this mess. "You're the hotshot pilot," he told his friend. "Do you know how to fly this type of cruiser?"

Anakin grabbed the controls. "You mean, do I know how to *land what's left* of this cruiser."

As the disintegrating ship plummeted, Anakin used the Force to help steady the ship and keep the damaged hull from burning up. With fire ships flanking them, Anakin guided the smoking wreck down to the planet's surface, skidding the crumbling frame across a flat area of Coruscant.

They made it! Once again Anakin was a hero.

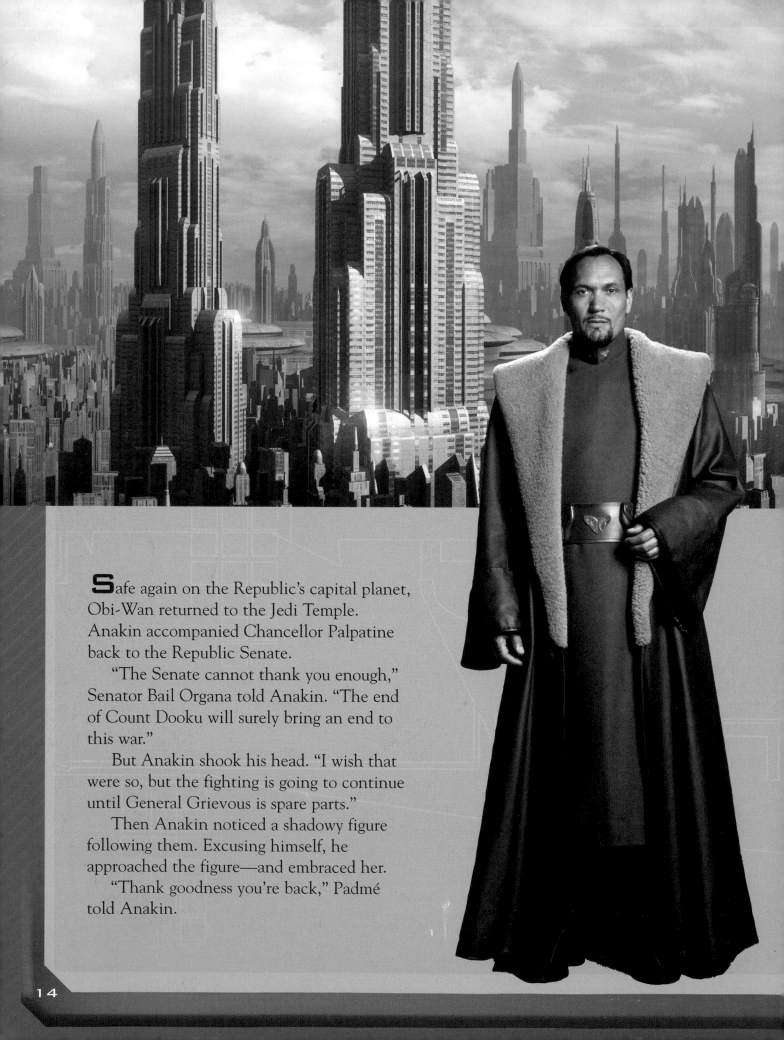

Safe again on the Republic's capital planet, Obi-Wan returned to the Jedi Temple. Anakin accompanied Chancellor Palpatine back to the Republic Senate.

"The Senate cannot thank you enough," Senator Bail Organa told Anakin. "The end of Count Dooku will surely bring an end to this war."

But Anakin shook his head. "I wish that were so, but the fighting is going to continue until General Grievous is spare parts."

Then Anakin noticed a shadowy figure following them. Excusing himself, he approached the figure—and embraced her.

"Thank goodness you're back," Padmé told Anakin.

Padmé Amidala was one of the Senate's most respected members. She was also Anakin's wife. For five months she'd waited for his return from a Jedi mission on the galaxy's Outer Rim. Now she could tell him her closely guarded secret—she was going to have a baby!

The news surprised Anakin. "That's wonderful," he said. But Padmé was worried. She knew the Jedi were forbidden to marry. Ever since their wedding ceremony on her home planet, Naboo, she and Anakin had kept their vows a secret. If the Jedi Council discovered Anakin was about to become a father, they would expel him from the Order.

"What are we going to do?" Padmé asked.

Anakin held her close. "It's going to be all right," he assured her. "We're not going to worry about anything right now. This is a happy moment. The happiest of my life."

General Grievous stepped off a shuttle on Utapau, a sinkhole planet with intricate cities built in caves deep in its underground walls. He hurried to the grand chamber of the Separatist Council.

The Council was made up of alien leaders who represented many groups trying to break away from the Republic. For years these Separatists had been waging a galaxy-wide civil war. At the moment, Grievous was in charge of their droid armies.

"It won't be long before the Republic army tracks us here," the general warned the Separatists. "Make your way to the Mustafar system on the Outer Rim. You will be safe there."

As the Separatist leaders departed, the hologram of a hooded figure appeared in the room. General Grievous immediately bowed to the shimmering image of the Sith Lord, Darth Sidious.

"The end of the war is near," announced Sidious, "and I promise you, victory is assured."

Sidious was the true mastermind behind the war against the Republic. Count Dooku had merely been his servant.

General Grievous was surprised to hear his Master say that the end of the war was coming, considering their recent defeat at the hands of the Jedi.

"But the loss of Count Dooku?" Grievous asked.

Sidious waved his hand. "The death of Count Dooku was a necessary loss. I will soon have a new apprentice . . . one far younger and more powerful."

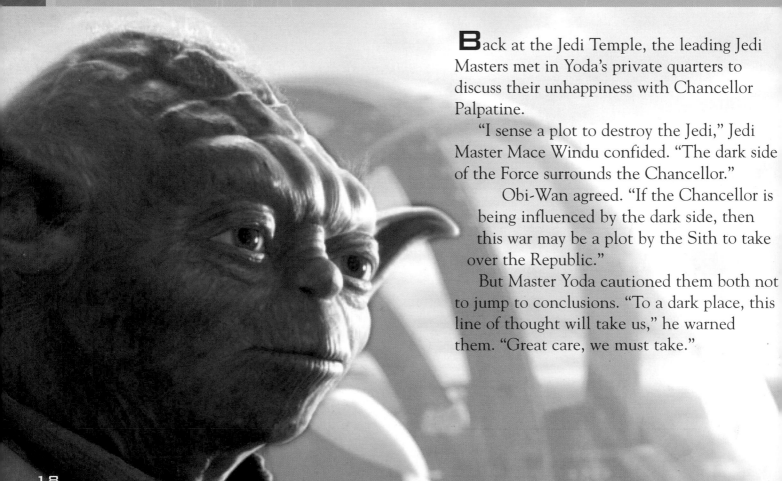

Back at the Jedi Temple, the leading Jedi Masters met in Yoda's private quarters to discuss their unhappiness with Chancellor Palpatine.

"I sense a plot to destroy the Jedi," Jedi Master Mace Windu confided. "The dark side of the Force surrounds the Chancellor."

Obi-Wan agreed. "If the Chancellor is being influenced by the dark side, then this war may be a plot by the Sith to take over the Republic."

But Master Yoda cautioned them both not to jump to conclusions. "To a dark place, this line of thought will take us," he warned them. "Great care, we must take."

Later that day, Chancellor Palpatine asked Anakin Skywalker to serve as his personal representative on the Jedi Council.

Anakin was thrilled with this honor, until he heard what his Jedi elders had to say. Although they granted him permission to sit on their Council, they refused to advance him to the level of Jedi Master.

"What?" Anakin cried angrily. "How can you do this? It's unfair . . . I'm more powerful than any of you!"

The Jedi Masters were embarrassed by Anakin's outburst. Anger, pride, lack of self-control—these were not the traits of a Jedi Master. The elders knew that Anakin still had much to learn.

"Take your seat, young Skywalker," Mace Windu sternly told him.

Quietly, Anakin took his seat, but deep down he was furious. He believed his heroic achievements had earned him the right to advancement. And he couldn't shake the idea that Chancellor Palpatine thought more of him than these jealous Jedi Masters!

After the Council meeting, Anakin confronted Obi-Wan. "What kind of nonsense is this? Put me on the Council and not make me a Master?"

Obi-Wan frowned. "Anakin, I worry when you speak from jealousy and pride. Those are not Jedi thoughts. They're dangerous, dark thoughts."

"Master, you of all people should have confidence in my abilities," protested Anakin. "I know where my loyalties lie."

Obi-Wan suspected it was time to find out. After a deep breath, he confided, "The Council wants you to report on all of the Chancellor's dealings. They want to know what he's up to."

Anakin was outraged. "They want me to *spy* on the Chancellor? That's treason!"

But Obi-Wan warned the young Knight that the Jedi Council suspected the Chancellor of treason himself.

Anakin wouldn't hear it. "The Chancellor is not a bad man."

Obi-Wan disagreed. "Use your feelings, Anakin. Something is out of place here."

Anakin shook his head. "You're asking me to do something against a mentor . . . and a friend. *That's* what's out of place here."

That night, Chancellor Palpatine asked Anakin to meet with him at the Galaxies Opera House. When the young Jedi entered the Chancellor's private box, Palpatine conveyed good news. Clone intelligence units had discovered General Grievous's location—he was hiding on the planet Utapau.

"At last," said Anakin, pleased. "He won't escape us this time."

Palpatine nodded and told his aides, "Leave us." He invited Anakin to sit down next to him, then leaned in close.

Anakin sensed that he and the Chancellor were about to have an important conversation—perhaps the most important of his life.

"Anakin," Palpatine began, "the Jedi Council wants control of the Republic. They're planning to betray me."

Anakin knew it was true. "I have to admit, my trust in them has been shaken," he confessed.

Palpatine seemed pleased to hear this. "The Jedi point of view is not the only valid one," he said. "The Dark Lords of the Sith believe in security and justice also . . . the Sith and Jedi are similar in almost every way. The difference between the two is the Sith are not afraid of the dark side of the Force. That is why they are more powerful."

Anakin was confused. He told Palpatine that he'd always been taught that the Jedi were selfless, using their powers only to help others, while the Sith were selfish, using their powers only to help themselves.

But Palpatine said this wasn't true. He told Anakin about a Sith Lord who had achieved such great knowledge of the dark side that he could even keep the ones he cared about from dying.

This astounded Anakin. Lately he had been plagued by nightmares of Padmé dying. He would do anything to keep his wife safe. "Is it possible to learn this power?" he asked Palpatine eagerly.

A tiny smile touched Palpatine's lips. "Not from a Jedi."

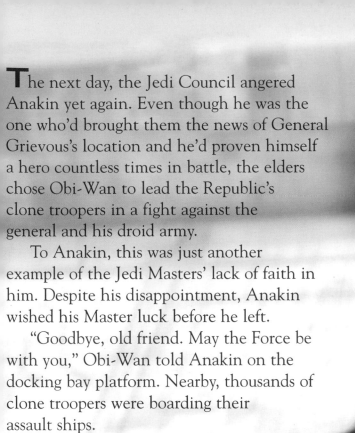

The next day, the Jedi Council angered Anakin yet again. Even though he was the one who'd brought them the news of General Grievous's location and he'd proven himself a hero countless times in battle, the elders chose Obi-Wan to lead the Republic's clone troopers in a fight against the general and his droid army.

To Anakin, this was just another example of the Jedi Masters' lack of faith in him. Despite his disappointment, Anakin wished his Master luck before he left.

"Goodbye, old friend. May the Force be with you," Obi-Wan told Anakin on the docking bay platform. Nearby, thousands of clone troopers were boarding their assault ships.

"May the Force be with you," replied Anakin.

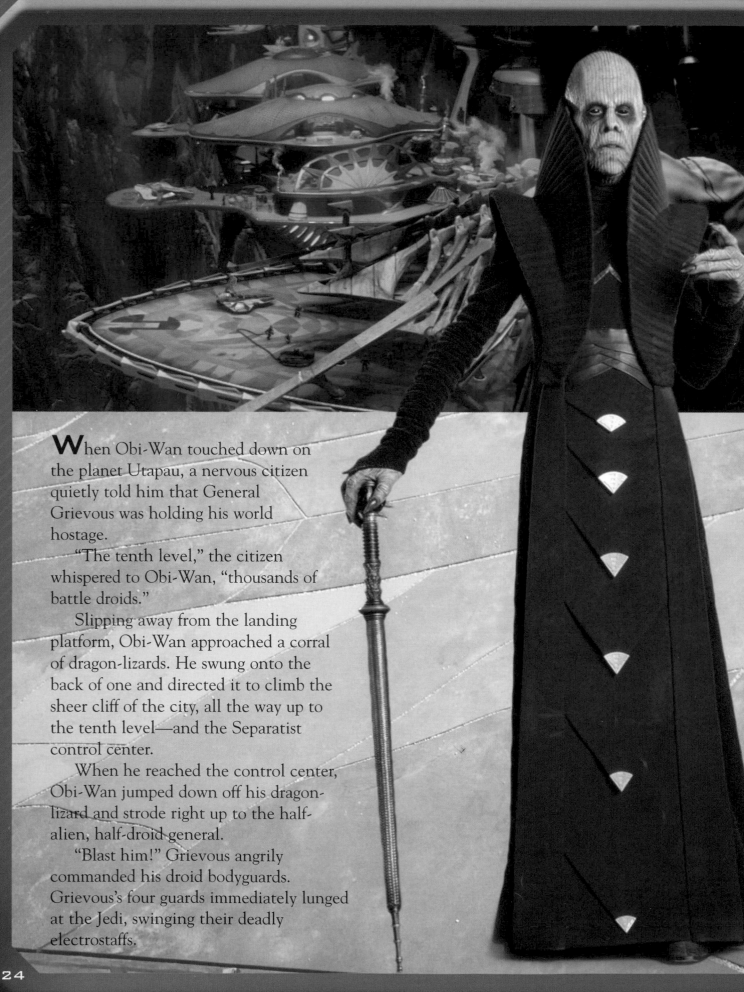

When Obi-Wan touched down on
the planet Utapau, a nervous citizen
quietly told him that General
Grievous was holding his world
hostage.

"The tenth level," the citizen
whispered to Obi-Wan, "thousands of
battle droids."

Slipping away from the landing
platform, Obi-Wan approached a corral
of dragon-lizards. He swung onto the
back of one and directed it to climb the
sheer cliff of the city, all the way up to
the tenth level—and the Separatist
control center.

When he reached the control center,
Obi-Wan jumped down off his dragon-
lizard and strode right up to the half-
alien, half-droid general.

"Blast him!" Grievous angrily
commanded his droid bodyguards.
Grievous's four guards immediately lunged
at the Jedi, swinging their deadly
electrostaffs.

Calling on the Force, Obi-Wan easily parried their clumsy blows. He brought the heavy roof down on one of the guards. With a few flashing sweeps of his lightsaber, he swiftly cut down the others. When the smoke cleared, General Grievous faced the Jedi alone.

"Attack, Kenobi!" Grievous commanded. "I have been trained in your Jedi arts by Count Dooku himself."

The general's arms separated. Grabbing four lightsabers from his belt, he struck! The four-armed assault drove Obi-Wan back, all the way across the control center.

Focusing his Jedi powers, Obi-Wan mounted a counterattack. His lightsaber whirled with lethal precision, and he deftly eliminated all of the general's weapons. But just as Obi-Wan was about to deal Grievous a fatal blow, destroyer droids struck!

The general's droids opened fire on Obi-Wan, but their mechanized targeting could not hit the elusive Jedi Master. Once again Obi-Wan had slid out of range.

"What are you trying to accomplish here?" Grievous shouted in frustration. "I have thousands of troops. You will not defeat them."

"I may not defeat your droids," declared Obi-Wan, "but my troops certainly will."

Just then, a loud explosion shook the room. With blaster rifles blazing, dozens of clone troopers dropped into the control center. Grievous fled, and Obi-Wan chased him out of the control center and into the city.

Laser bolts flew all around Obi-Wan as the Republic's clone troopers waged war on the Separatists' droid army. Finally Obi-Wan caught up with Grievous on a secret landing platform, where the cyborg general brutally turned on the Jedi. Obi-Wan had no choice but to stop Grievous for good, firing a fatal shot with the general's own blaster pistol.

"Contact Coruscant," Obi-Wan told his trusted trooper, Clone Commander Cody. "Tell them General Grievous has been destroyed."

Meanwhile, back on Coruscant, Chancellor Palpatine was revealing something very important to Anakin.

"My mentor taught me everything about the Force," the Chancellor confessed, "even the nature of the dark side."

Anakin's eyes widened. "You're a Sith Lord!"

"I am a Sith Lord," Palpatine admitted.

Anakin was stunned by this admission. Since he'd been a young boy, Palpatine had been a loyal leader of the Republic. How could he be a Sith? An enemy of the Jedi?

"I am not your enemy, Anakin," Palpatine quickly told him. "I need your help to restore peace in the galaxy. . . . The Jedi are plotting to take over the Republic. They plan to destroy me . . . and eventually destroy you."

Anakin shook his head. He did not wish to betray Palpatine, but he could not ignore his duty as a Jedi. "I will quickly discover the truth of all this," he said. Then Anakin left the Chancellor's office and went straight to the Jedi Temple.

After Anakin told the Jedi Council what he'd just learned, Mace Windu ordered him to remain at the Temple. Then Mace and three other Jedi Masters went straight to the Chancellor's office.

"In the name of the Galactic Senate of the Republic," said Mace, "you are under arrest." Mace and his fellow Jedi Masters drew their lightsabers.

But the Jedi Masters had uncovered more than a simple traitor—they'd unveiled the darkest Sith Lord of all. As Darth Sidious, Palpatine had helped twist the galaxy into chaos by creating a civil war. Now his deadly Sith powers would be unleashed on the Jedi who dared to challenge him.

Palpatine moved a hidden lightsaber down his sleeve and into his hand, igniting its glowing red blade.

In a flash, Palpatine struck down Masters Saesee Tiin and Agen Kolar. Next he turned on Kit Fisto and Mace Windu. In seconds, Kit was cut down, too!

Palpatine launched himself at Mace Windu. They dueled ferociously. In the heat of battle, Mace slashed a window, sending it twenty stories to the ground. Palpatine pressed Mace onto the ledge. But the Jedi Master quickly knocked Palpatine's lightsaber across the floor.

"You are well versed in the ways of the Jedi, my Lord," Mace told Palpatine, "but you are no Jedi!"

Palpatine's eyes flared. He raised his hand and Force lightning flew from his fingers. Mace blocked the searing blue bolts of energy with his lightsaber, but the assault was overwhelming.

Just then, Anakin raced into the room. He had disobeyed Mace's order to remain at the Jedi Temple. Now the young Knight stood paralyzed by the sight before his eyes.

"Anakin, help me!" cried Mace, struggling to hold back the lethal blue rays.

Drawing his lightsaber, Anakin rushed to help the Jedi Master.

"Don't!" shouted Palpatine. "He's a traitor! He'll betray you just as he betrayed me. You're not one of them, Anakin."

With a powerful effort, Mace forced Palpatine's hands to arch backward. The Chancellor's face began to twist and distort, and his eyes became yellow. In another moment, Palpatine would be pushed off the window ledge.

Anakin was torn. Palpatine was a Sith Lord, but he had always been a loyal friend and mentor to him. He couldn't stand by and watch his friend die!

"I am your pathway to power, Anakin! Help me!" Palpatine begged.

Anakin lunged forward and struck, cutting off Mace's lightsaber hand. Instantly the Sith Lord's Force lightning engulfed the Jedi Master, driving Mace Windu out the window and to his death.

"What have I done? What have I done?" cried Anakin. For a moment he felt stunned. How could he have helped to murder a Jedi?

But Palpatine immediately soothed the young man's conscience. "You're following your destiny," he assured Anakin. "The Jedi are traitors. You saved the Republic . . . and what about Padmé? I can help you protect her. Become my apprentice. Learn to use the dark side of the Force."

Anakin considered Palpatine's words. Anakin's worries about Padmé were unrelenting. To protect her, he'd do anything. *Anything.* "I do . . . I do want your knowledge," Anakin admitted. "I want the power to stop death."

"Good. Good!" said Palpatine.

"You were right," Anakin said at last. "The Jedi betrayed both of us." Slowly he knelt before Palpatine. "I pledge myself to your care . . . to the ways of the Sith."

"Anakin Skywalker, you are one with the Order of the Sith Lords. Henceforth," declared Palpatine, "you shall be known as Darth . . . Vader."

"Thank you, my Master," Anakin found himself saying. The words were too easy. And now it was done.

"Rise, Darth Vader," said Palpatine, an evil smile touching his lips. Now that Palpatine had twisted Anakin to his will, he sent him to the Jedi Temple. The Jedi were the enemy now, he told Anakin, and they had to be destroyed. All of them.

"Do what must be done, Lord Vader," said Palpatine. "Show no mercy."

While his new dark apprentice headed for the Jedi Temple, Palpatine focused on the remaining Jedi on missions across the galaxy. By comlink transmission, Palpatine activated a deadly code that had been secretly implanted in the Republic's clone commanders long ago.

"The time has come," Palpatine told his commanders. "Execute Order Sixty-six."

On the planet Utapau, Clone Commander Cody nodded at his comlink. "It will be done, my Lord," he said. The commander signed off and began to search for his Jedi general, Obi-Wan Kenobi.

"**I** have a bad feeling about this," said Obi-Wan when he saw his own clone troops begin to fire on him.

As laser blasts engulfed him, Obi-Wan jumped off the edge of a sinkhole and dove hundreds of feet to the water below. Using his breathing device, he hid until the shooting stopped. Then he swiftly swam to the surface. He made his way to General Grievous's secret landing platform and escaped in the general's waiting starfighter.

Across the galaxy, other Jedi were not as lucky as Obi-Wan. Again and again, Jedi Knights and Masters were caught off guard and struck down by their own troops.

On the Wookiee home planet, Kashyyyk, Jedi Master Yoda had been leading his clones in a fight against a battle droid invasion. Suddenly, in the midst of his meditations, Yoda's eyes snapped open. "Something is wrong," he told his two Wookiee bodyguards, Chewbacca and Tarfful. "Stay alert."

Clone Commander Gree entered the room with eight officers and struck! Using his lightsaber, Yoda deflected their laser fire, then cut down his attackers with agility and power.

Chewbacca and Tarfful fired their weapons as more clones charged them. Outside, a clone officer commanded a Republic tank to fire, and the entire building went up in flames. But not before the Wookiees helped Yoda slip away to an escape craft.

"Chewbacca and Tarfful, good friends you are," Yoda told the Wookiees. "For your help, much gratitude and respect, I have."

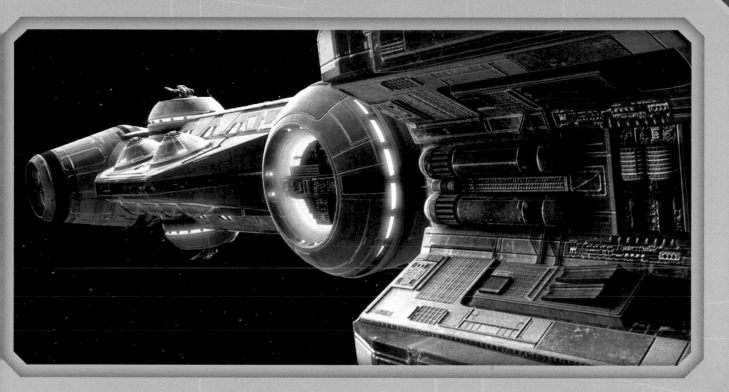

Yoda and Obi-Wan Kenobi were finally reunited when Senator Bail Organa signaled their ships and brought them aboard his Alderaan starcruiser.

"You were attacked by your clones, also?" Obi-Wan asked Yoda.

Yoda nodded. "With the help of the Wookiees, barely escape, I did."

"How many more Jedi managed to survive?" asked Obi-Wan.

"We've heard from none," Yoda told him.

Bail Organa then explained what he'd witnessed back on Coruscant. "I saw black smoke coming from the Jedi Temple. There were signs of a terrible battle. Something is seriously wrong. That's why I went looking for Yoda."

The trio realized a coded signal was being sent out of the Jedi Temple, commanding all Jedi to return.

"We have to go back," Obi-Wan insisted. "If there are other stragglers, they will fall into the trap and be killed."

"It's too dangerous," warned Bail.

But Yoda knew Obi-Wan was right. Not only did they need to dismantle the coded signal, they needed to find out what had happened and why.

"The attempt on my life has left me scarred and deformed," Palpatine announced to the vast Senate Chamber later that day. "But the remaining Jedi will be hunted down and destroyed."

All afternoon Palpatine had been presenting evidence to the Senate of what he claimed was a Jedi plot to overthrow the Republic. Now the Senators were madly applauding Palpatine, believing he had saved their lives.

"We stand on the threshold of a new beginning," Palpatine told them. "The Republic will be reorganized into the first Galactic Empire, which, I assure you, will last for ten thousand years. An empire that will be ruled by a sovereign ruler, chosen for life. . . ."

As cheers rose through the Chamber, Senator Bail Organa joined Senator Padmé Amidala in her Senate box. Both were outraged by what they'd just heard. Palpatine was dissolving the Republic's democracy and making himself *Emperor*!

"So this is how liberty dies," Padmé said in stunned disbelief. "With thunderous applause. . . ."

Not far away, Yoda and Obi-Wan snuck into the Jedi Temple's main control center. After Obi-Wan reprogrammed the coded signal to warn any surviving Jedi to stay away, he turned to Yoda.

"I must know the truth," said Obi-Wan, and he played a hologram recording of what had taken place there earlier.

As Obi-Wan and Yoda watched, a nightmarish scene began. A familiar figure was using his lightsaber to strike down a class of Jedi younglings.

Obi-Wan was devastated. "It can't be . . . ," he whispered. But it was. The murderous figure in the hologram recording was Anakin Skywalker. After the terrible carnage, a dark robed figure entered the room and approached Anakin. Obi-Wan's former apprentice knelt before the figure.

"The traitors have been destroyed, Lord Sidious," Anakin declared.

"You have done well, my new apprentice," Emperor Palpatine replied.

Turning away, Obi-Wan said, "I can't watch any more."

Yoda shook his head. "Destroy the Sith, we must."

"Send me to kill the Emperor," said Obi-Wan. "I will not kill Anakin."

"Twisted by the dark side, young Skywalker has become," said Yoda. "The boy you trained, gone, he is. Consumed by Darth Vader. Use your feelings, Obi-Wan, and find him, you will. Visit the new Emperor, my task is. May the Force be with you."

When Yoda entered the Emperor's Senate office, Palpatine attacked with a barrage of Force lightning. The crackling blue energy bolts slammed into Yoda, throwing the tiny Jedi through the air and into a wall.

"I have waited a long time for this moment, my little green friend," said Palpatine with a chuckle. "At last the Sith Lords will rule the galaxy."

Exploding from his crumpled position, Yoda rocketed into Palpatine, knocking his body clear over the desk. "Not if anything I have to say about it, Lord Sidious," said Master Yoda, igniting his lightsaber.

Lightsabers blazed and the duel began. Palpatine called upon his dark arts, slashing away in fury, but Yoda's accomplished command of the Force blocked his every blow.

Overmatched, Palpatine fled into the vast Senate Chamber. He rushed into a control pod and it began to rise from the floor. Then Yoda leaped aboard, unleashing a masterful assault.

Palpatine fired back a devastating array of Force lightning, then called another pod to him and jumped for it. Yoda tried to follow, but another bolt of searing energy struck him—and sent him plunging down hundreds of meters to the Chamber floor.

Palpatine immediately ordered clone troopers to search for Yoda's body. But they found no sign of it. The Jedi Master had disappeared.

Crawling through the Senate's narrow wiring chutes, Yoda hailed Bail Organa through his comlink. Bail piloted his speeder close to the Senate building's outer wall, then signaled Yoda to drop down through a light-fixture opening.

"Failed, I have," said Yoda sadly.

But, thanks to the Alderaan Senator, the tiny Master had escaped to fight another day. . . .

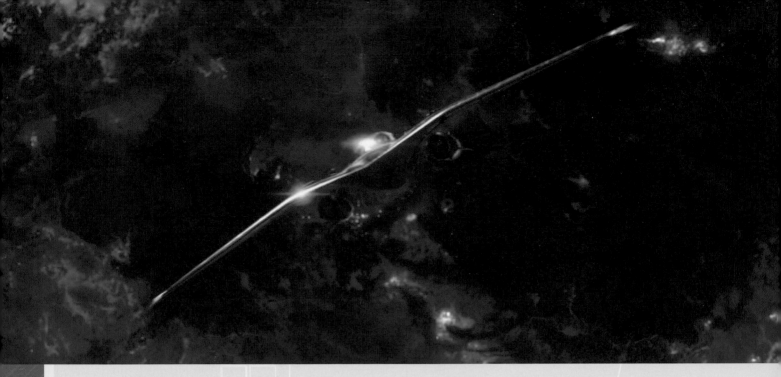

Meanwhile, in another part of the galaxy, a Naboo cruiser touched down amid the churning volcanoes of the planet Mustafar. Senator Padmé Amidala rushed across the landing platform to greet her husband.

Anakin had come to Mustafar on Emperor Palpatine's orders. He'd already completed his mission, executing every one of the Separatist leaders to end the trumped-up civil war.

Now Padmé confronted her husband about the terrible things he'd done. Obi-Wan Kenobi had told her everything. But she had to hear it from Anakin himself.

"He said you have turned to the dark side," Padmé cried, "that you killed younglings."

Anakin was outraged. "Obi-Wan is trying to turn you against me."

"No!" protested Padmé. She'd come here hoping to save Anakin, to turn him back into the man she loved, but it was too late. When Anakin saw Obi-Wan emerge from Padmé's ship, he jumped to a terrible conclusion.

"You're with him. You've betrayed me!" he cried.

"No!" Padmé insisted. But Anakin's dark heart wouldn't listen. Reaching out, he began to choke his wife.

"Let her go, Anakin," said Obi-Wan, stepping forward. As the Jedi Master advanced, Anakin released Padmé, tossing her across the platform. Unconscious, she crumpled to the floor.

Anakin threw off his cloak. "You will not take her from me," he told Obi-Wan.

"Your anger and your lust for power have already done that," said Obi-Wan. "You've let the Dark Lord twist your point of view. Now you're the very thing you swore to destroy."

"Don't make me kill you," warned Anakin.

Obi-Wan ignited his lightsaber. "I will do what I must."

"You will try, my old friend," Anakin declared, igniting his own lightsaber.

Lashing out, Anakin began the most ferocious fight of his life. Sparks flew as the two former friends worked their way across the landing platform and into a control room. Anakin's thrusts were savage, and Obi-Wan was constantly on the defensive. But the Jedi Master soon gained the upper hand, knocking Anakin off balance and seizing his lightsaber.

"The flaw of power is arrogance," warned Obi-Wan, standing over Anakin. Gathering the will to strike, the Jedi Master gazed at the young man he'd mentored for so many years.

"You hesitate," taunted Anakin. "The flaw of *compassion*."

In a flash, Anakin grabbed Obi-Wan's wrists, holding both lightsabers at bay. The two struggled, but Anakin had grown too strong. Obi-Wan was forced to release Anakin's weapon.

Anakin lunged, driving Obi-Wan down a narrow balcony—to its very edge. Obi-Wan peered over the end at a river of lava. As Anakin pressed his advance, Obi-Wan had no choice but to tightrope-walk along a small pipe extending out over the molten abyss.

The pipe ended at the main collection plant, where Obi-Wan and Anakin jumped from level to level. Sparks flew as their crackling blades crossed again and again. A huge spray of white-hot lava shot up, raining on the two and burning them.

The terrible duel finally brought them to the bank of the lava river, where Obi-Wan gained the upper hand. With swift blows, he crippled Anakin, who tumbled down the embankment and rolled to a stop at the river's scorching edge.

Anakin struggled to pull himself up, but his injuries were too great. "Help me, Master," he desperately pleaded.

"Don't ask me, Anakin," said Obi-Wan, his heart full of pain. "You were my brother, Anakin. I love you, but I won't help you."

"I hate you!" Anakin shouted. A moment later, the heat of the lava had reached him and he burst into flames.

Believing Darth Vader to be dead, Obi-Wan turned away.

Close by, an Imperial shuttle was just landing. Palpatine had arrived! Obi-Wan ran back to Padmé's ship. C-3PO, Padmé's protocol droid, informed Obi-Wan that he'd already carried Padmé aboard, and they quickly fled.

Clone troopers accompanied Emperor Palpatine off the shuttle. When they found Anakin's smoldering form, Palpatine leaned over him. "He's still alive," he told the clones. "Get a medical capsule immediately." Then the Sith Lord placed a hand on Anakin's forehead.

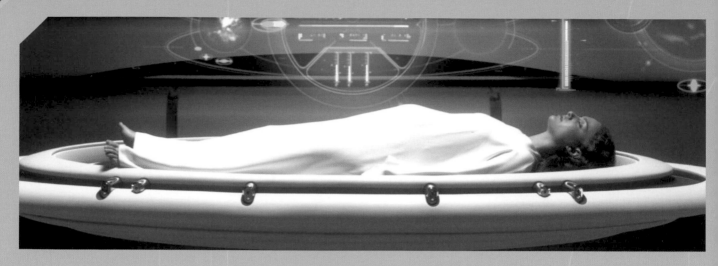

"**M**edically, she is completely healthy. For reasons we can't explain, we are losing her."

The medical droid's words shocked Obi-Wan, Bail, and Yoda. The three had been waiting patiently outside the operating room for word of Padmé's condition.

"She's dying?" asked Obi-Wan in disbelief.

"She has lost the will to live," said the medical droid. "We need to operate quickly if we are to save the babies."

"Babies!" cried Bail in surprise.

"She's carrying twins," said the medical droid before rushing back to the operating room.

As the twins were delivered, Obi-Wan took Padmé's hand. "You have twins, Padmé," Obi-Wan told her.

She told him to name the girl Leia and the boy Luke. "They need you . . . hang on," Obi-Wan said.

With tears in her eyes, the former Queen and rebel, Senator and fighter, shook her head. "I can't . . . ," she whispered, and on her dying breath she said, "Obi-Wan, there is good in him. I know there is . . . still."

With Padmé gone, Anakin's twin babies were in great danger.

"Hidden, safe, the children must be kept," said Yoda. He knew that Emperor Palpatine would try to harm them—or claim them and attempt to turn them to the dark side.

Obi-Wan agreed. "Someplace where the Sith will not sense their presence."

"Split up, they should be," Yoda decided.

"My wife and I will take the girl," offered Senator Bail Organa. "She will be loved with us."

"And what about the boy?" asked Obi-Wan.

"To Tatooine," declared Yoda.

Obi-Wan nodded. "I will take the child and watch over him." After a pause, Obi-Wan finally asked, "Master Yoda, do you think Anakin's twins will be able to defeat Darth Sidious?"

Yoda had already considered this question. "Strong the Force runs, in the Skywalker line," he said. "Only hope, we can. Done then, it is. Until the time is right, disappear, we will."

"My Lord, construction is finished," the Emperor's medical droid announced to Palpatine. "He lives."

Because of his massive burn injuries, Darth Vader awakened in an Imperial medical center to find himself enrobed in a dark prison—one he would be forced to endure for the rest of his life. A heavy suit of airtight armor covered his body, and his face was sealed in a terrifying mask.

Desperately Vader asked about Padmé. "Is she all right?"

"I'm afraid she died," Palpatine informed him. "It seems in your anger, you killed her."

As Vader's agonizing screams echoed through the building's corridors, Palpatine secretly smiled. Vader's rage and pain could be channeled into the kind of vengeful power that would strike fear into an entire galaxy.

Yes, thought Palpatine. *My carefully laid plans are realized at last.*

Anakin Skywalker was the most powerful Jedi who ever lived. With his turn to the dark side complete, nothing and no one could stop the Emperor now.

But the evil Sith Lord was wrong.

In another part of the galaxy, an escape pod landed on the remote planet Dagobah. It was the perfect sanctuary for Jedi Master Yoda. Here he could evade his enemies, continue to study the Jedi arts, and patiently wait for the children of Anakin and Padmé to grow old enough to realize their destiny.

Someday, the gifted Skywalker twins would need him—and when that day came, Yoda would be ready.

While Anakin's baby daughter, Leia, was secretly placed in the arms of Alderaan's Queen, Anakin's son, Luke, was taken to the remote desert world of Tatooine. There Obi-Wan entrusted the boy to Anakin's stepbrother, Owen Lars. He agreed to raise the child in secret.

As Tatooine's twin suns set, Obi-Wan sadly bid goodbye to Luke, but he knew their parting would not be forever.

Many years from now, Luke and Leia Skywalker, offspring of the most powerful Jedi who ever lived, would understand their true destiny. Obi-Wan knew the Jedi and all they stood for were not dead.

In these children, a new hope was born. . . .

Little Bear's Shapes

JANE HISSEY

RED FOX

square   circle   triangle   rectangle   star   semi-circle

square

square flag

Little Bear's
Shapes

cube sphere pyramid cone cuboid cylinder

The toys are cutting out square windows.

square circle triangle rectangle star semi-circle

circle

blue circle

Bruno's wooden hoop is a circle.

square   circle   **triangle**   rectangle   star   semi-circle

triangle

red triangle

cube sphere pyramid cone cuboid cylinder

Little Bear's dragon mask has triangles for teeth.

square　　　circle　　　triangle　　　rectangle　　　star　　　semi-circle

rectangle

See-through rectangle

cube   sphere   pyramid   cone   cuboid   cylinder

The bears are all holding paper rectangles.

square   circle   triangle   rectangle   star   semi-circle

star

paper star

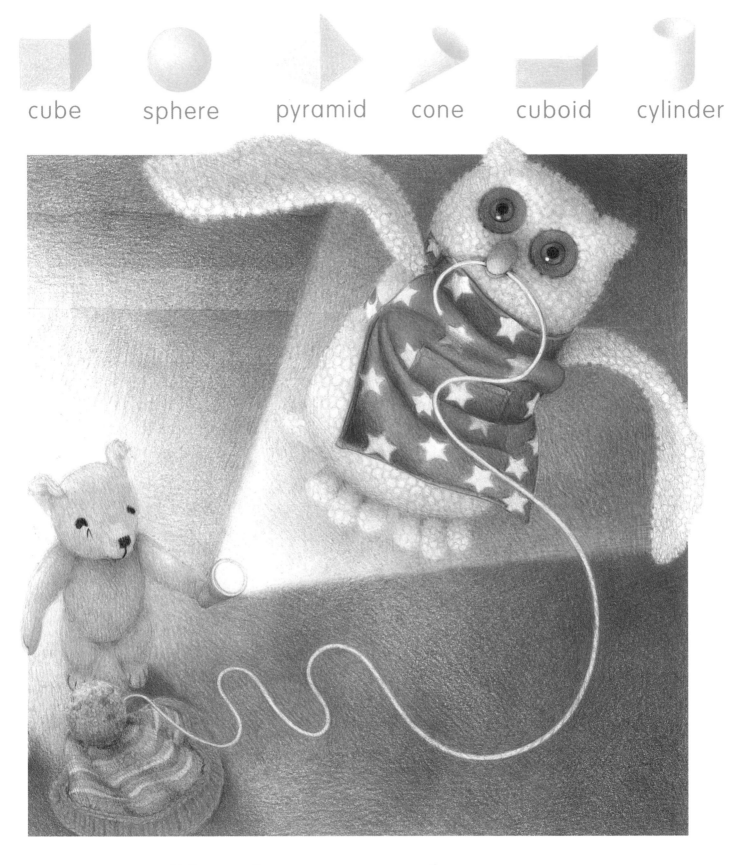

| cube | sphere | pyramid | cone | cuboid | cylinder |

Hoot has stars on her apron.

square　　circle　　triangle　　rectangle　　star　　semi-circle

semi-circle

biscuit semi-circles

cube   sphere   pyramid   cone   cuboid   cylinder

Bramwell is pointing to a yellow semi-circle.

These are all two-dimensional –
2-D – shapes. They are flat.

These are all three-dimensional –
3-D – shapes. They are not flat.

square   circle   triangle   rectangle   star   semi-circle

cube

wooden cubes

cube   sphere   pyramid   cone   cuboid   cylinder

Ruff's birthday cake is a cube.

sphere

glass sphere

cube **sphere** pyramid cone cuboid cylinder

The ball the toys have found is a sphere.

square   circle   triangle   rectangle   star   semi-circle

pyramid

green pyramid

cube   sphere   **pyramid**   cone   cuboid   cylinder

Camel is galloping past some pyramids.

square   circle   triangle   rectangle   star   semi-circle

cone

ice-cream cones

cube   sphere   pyramid   **cone**   cuboid   cylinder

Little Bear and Ruff have cone-shaped hats.

cuboid

cuboid suitcase

Sarah Elizabeth's sewing box is a cuboid.

square

circle

triangle

rectangle

star

semi-circle

cylinder

wooden cylinder

cube   sphere   pyramid   cone   cuboid   cylinder

Bramwell's rolling pin is a cylinder.

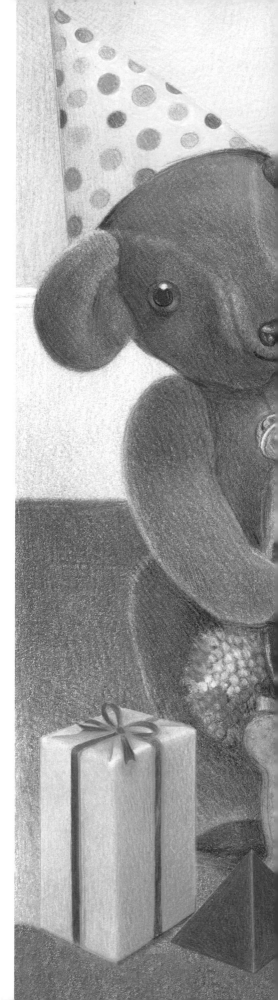

How many shapes can you find?

LITTLE BEAR'S SHAPES
A RED FOX BOOK 0 09 943928 X

Published in Great Britain by arrangement with Hutchinson,
an imprint of Random House Children's Books

This edition published 2002

1 3 5 7 9 10 8 6 4 2

© Jane Hissey 2002

Red Fox Books are published by Random House Children's Books,
61–63 Uxbridge Road, London W5 5SA,
a division of The Random House Group Ltd,
in Australia by Random House Australia (Pty) Ltd,
20 Alfred Street, Milsons Point, Sydney, NSW 2061, Australia,
in New Zealand by Random House New Zealand Ltd,
18 Poland Road, Glenfield, Auckland 10, New Zealand,
and in South Africa by Random House (Pty) Ltd,
Endulini, 5A Jubilee Road, Parktown 2193, South Africa

THE RANDOM HOUSE GROUP Limited Reg. No. 954009
www.kidsatrandomhouse.co.uk

A CIP catalogue record for this book is available from the British Library.

Printed in Singapore by Tien Wah Press [PTE] Ltd